SANTA
baby

Published by Bliss Ink, Chelle Bliss, and Eden Butler
Published on November 27 th 2019
Edited by Silently Correcting Your Grammar
Proofread by Julie Deaton
Cover © Chelle Bliss

MAGGIE

The gas gauge was nearing E, and there was only one dollar left from the tips I managed to scrape together after my shift. The snow was thicker here in this small, no-name town. This wasn't Bronxville like I thought. I'd missed my exit and was at least two towns from where I needed to be.

I'd never make it to my aunt's. In reality, I wouldn't make it another mile. Not with the snow, a snoring baby, and no money to get me there.

I had to face facts. I was lost. Stuck in

some Hallmark-movie version of Little Italy. I gazed out the windshield, taking in the twinkling Christmas lights, and sigh. The only thing making this town remotely shady was my secondhand rust bucket of a car. It was idling on the street across from a cozy-looking restaurant that, from the looks of it, the entire town seemed to be at in celebration.

Everyone but me.

Because I was stranded.

And lost.

And a little pathetic.

Because my boss was an idiot.

Kip, the diner's manager, didn't care that my sitter flaked out on me. He didn't care that I was left with a sick six-month-old with three hours left in the busiest part of the Christmas Eve rush. Kip only cared that Mateo, my sweet son, was crying loud enough to disturb the customers.

"Shut him up, Maggie, or get the fuck out of my diner," the asshole who made the Grinch seem sweet yelled at me.

"But..." I needed half an hour to get him calm, then Vi, another waitress, would finish her shift and take him off my hands. But Kip didn't care about anything but the rush and the baby crying in my arms.

"I just need…"

"You need to go home and take that screaming brat with you."

He wouldn't get my tears. "What about my tips…and my check?"

"You can square that up on your next shift." He winced as Mateo's crying grew louder, his shoulders curling as if the sound of a baby's cry was going to make his ears bleed.

"Kip, I need that money to get back to my aunt's tonight," I begged, rocking Mateo, hoping to quiet him.

"Not my problem," Kip growled, making me flinch.

Mateo seemed to pick up on my fear and screamed louder, his sobs drawing the attention of the customers. Kip threw up his hands and hurried into his office, slamming the door in my face before I could make him see reason.

"Ay, Dios mío …" I whispered, staring at the door, my eyes growing wet, my heart pounding.

"You all right, sugar?" Vi's soft, rasping voice sounded over Mateo's cries.

I turned, blinking quickly to keep myself from crying. "Kip's just being…"

She'd always been so sweet to me. Like a mother—or, from the looks of her white hair and deeply lined face, grandmother was probably more accurate. But Vi had her own troubles. Everyone did. She didn't need any of mine.

"A rotten prick?" The older lady shook her head as she glared at the closed door. "Always has been, always will be." She tugged her purse over her shoulder, glancing down at Mateo's red face, her focus on the way he pulled at his ear. "He's teething."

"What?" I asked, peering down at my son.

Vi nodded, touching the baby's chin to open his mouth. "Run your finger over his gums."

Mateo went quiet at my touch. There were

two small ridges that scraped against my fingertip, making me wince.

Vi smiled, brushing the thick hair from his forehead. "Get him a teething ring. If you can't afford that, stick a wet rag in the freezer, and when it's ready, let him chew on it. If that doesn't work, dip the damn thing in some whiskey. It won't hurt him and might give him and you a little relief." She exhaled, staring at mijo like she'd never seen anything sweeter. "If you don't have any whiskey, I'll steal some from Albert when he passes out."

That would be bad for Vi. Her husband was the kind of drunk who probably kept a close eye on his stash.

Mateo calmed a little, his small body slumping against my chest as I followed Vi toward the door. "I didn't know you had kids."

"What I have is experience." She held the door open for me, helping me wrestle the nearly empty diaper bag and my exhausted baby into the twelve-year-old Monte Carlo at the back of the parking lot. Vi stood next to the car as I fastened

Mateo into his car seat and stuffed two thick quilts around him. When I shut the door, Vi frowned.

"What?"

"This car isn't safe," she said, shaking her head.

"It's all I got. You know that."

"That hole in the floor..." She pointed through the window, grimacing.

I dropped my shoulders, tired from my shift. "My cousin put down a piece of plywood and some epoxy. I just can't afford anything else right now, especially not if Kip keeps running my shifts."

"You could ask that piece of shit..."

"No, Vi," I interrupted, not disguising the clip in my tone. "I couldn't." I was always kind to Vi because she'd always been good to me. But I'd never relent on this one. She knew a little bit about why I was raising Mateo on my own—but not everything.

"You're so stubborn. The man has money."

The laugh I released held no humor. "He has

a habit, and I don't want Mateo around him." I rubbed my neck, pulling the edges of my coat together, wishing for the dozenth time I could afford one without missing buttons. "I don't want my son around a drug addict, no matter if he's his father or not."

Vi nodded, her face hardening for a second as she looked back at the diner, like there was something she wanted to say but wouldn't.

The snow had begun to fall around us and had started to collect on her shoulders, sticking in her thick white hair so I couldn't make out what was a flurry or a curl.

"You should go," I told her, squeezing her hand when she looked over my car, likely wondering if there was a single spot of the roof or around the bottom where rust hadn't begun to eat away at the metal. "We'll be fine."

"You have enough gas to get to your aunt's?"

I didn't, but if I admitted that, Vi would insist we come home with her or that I let her give me money. There was a faint purple bruise healing under her left eye, put there by the shittiest *husband any woman had ever had. I'd rather walk back to the city than risk her getting another one.*

"We'll be fine. I promise."

She began to argue, and I hurried to hug her, seeming to catch the woman off guard. She froze when I threw my arms around her, but then she relaxed, laughing when I wouldn't let go until she returned my embrace.

"Hell, Maggie, you're a good kid." She patted my back, shaking her head at my car one last time before she walked away.

My eyes hadn't left the gas gage as I drove away from the diner. I should have called my aunt and explained that I wouldn't be able to make it to see her for the holiday. There was no sense in risking the snow and my lack of funds on the off chance I might make it. But I'd done it before. Plenty of times. I'd gotten there on less. I convinced myself, at least.

I'm an idiot.

But I ached for my small family. They

were all I had left, and I wanted Mateo's first Christmas to be special. Even if he would never remember it, I still wanted him to have something nice like I did once.

Behind me, those little snores grew louder, and I looked over my shoulder, my heart aching at the roundness of his face and wide arch of his mouth. Why did he have to look so much like Alejandro?

The car was warm, but it wouldn't be for long. Soon, I'd have to find a phone and call my aunt. I'd have to admit defeat and find someone somewhere who would take pity on us. A glance around this pretty, clean town told me instantly there likely weren't any shelters. No. That wouldn't be good anyway.

We could wrap up in those blankets together...

Jesus, please don't let us freeze.

The thought tore apart the small threads of composure I'd been holding on to all night. The steering wheel was hot from the vent, and I gripped it tightly, keeping my forehead away from it as I let my tears fall, cursing Alejandro for being weak and breaking every promise he made to me. We were supposed to live our biggest dreams—dreams we'd invented when we were college freshmen falling in love, determined nothing would break us apart. But something had.

He had.

His weaknesses.

His excesses.

And I got left alone on Christmas Eve. With our baby…

"Hey." I heard, the voice loud, deep, the sound like a warning that had me jerking my head up to stare out my foggy window. I could only make out the wide-shouldered shape of a man and hear the rap of his knuckles against the glass when he knocked. "You in there?"

The sudden vision of a thousand

dark, twisted scenarios started to play in my head. Suddenly, this picturesque, sweet little town didn't seem all that wholesome. It was too quiet. Too deserted.

Another tap came, this one heavier, the rap like metal on glass, and I eased my hand to the door, hoping the man couldn't make out my movements through the foggy glass before I engaged the automatic locks. They, at least, still worked.

"You're testing my fucking patience. I'm asking one more time, and then I'm breaking the glass…" he said, punctuating his threat with another rap against the window.

I realized what the noise was when I wiped the glass clear, and my eyes widened. "Oh my God, please don't!" I held up my hands, already surrendering, my prayers silently firing off in quick succession. "Please! I'm…I'm unarmed!"

He leaned forward, his face coming into view, and I wondered how it was possible to be so terrified by someone so damn beautiful. The man had chiseled features, as though he stepped right out of an old black-and-white movie. His cheekbones were high, and his mouth was plump, his eyes squinting and searching over what I supposed was my petrified but curious expression.

"The fuck are you doing out here?"

"I…I'm just…" Mateo chose that exact moment to wake up, seeming to remember with a jolt that his little gums ached. "I'm sorry," I told the man, my hands still up as I slowly turned. "I…have to get my baby. I'm not doing anything bad. Honest!"

The man watched me as I pulled the baby from his car seat and grabbed him and the quilts, shushing him as I turned back to sit behind the wheel.

"It's okay, *mijo*," I told my son, rocking

him as best as I could while some strange man stared at me through the window, holding a gun.

"Why are you out here in the snow with a baby?"

I jerked my gaze to him, feeling a sudden rush of insult at the question, forgetting about the gun. "Is that your business?" I snapped. I was doing my best even though I was sure it didn't look that way.

He cocked an eyebrow, leaning the hand not holding the gun against my car. "Yeah, right now, it is."

"I…am almost out of gas, and the snow…" I waved at the clouds, then nodded at the street. He didn't follow my movements. Instead, the handsome man kept his attention on me and Mateo, his focus intensifying as my son's body stiffened each time he took a breath to gear up for another cry.

"He hungry?"

"Possibly," I said, positioning the baby at my breast before I stopped. I couldn't do this here. With an audience, out in the cold.

"Is there a problem?"

"I'm...fine," I told him, my fear quickly replaced by worry as Mateo's face heated and he took to pulling on his ear. He probably wouldn't nurse anyway. His gums were too sore, and he was in pain. What did Vi say? The frozen rag. "I just..." Glancing at the man, then to the crowd milling inside the restaurant, I decided my desperation outweighed any self-preservation I had. If this man were going to hurt me, he'd have done it by now.

"Can you back up a little?" I asked him, nodding toward the door. He hesitated for a second, but he didn't put up an argument. He watched me, his curious eyes relaxing when I rolled down the window.

It was a rash decision, but my baby was in pain and I was desperate. I pulled the small burp rag from the diaper bag, making sure it at least was clean, and unfolded it before I grabbed a handful of snow that had collected on the windshield. Then, I placed the snow in the rag and twisted it, making a pouch small enough to fit against Mateo's aching gums.

Several seconds passed before he took to it. I knew it was only a temporary remedy, but at least he would have some relief. Sure enough, after several long seconds, Mateo stopped fighting the intrusion of the frigid rag in his mouth and sucked on it, his small body relaxing.

"Clever woman," the man said, his voice even and the threat missing completely.

"Resourceful," I corrected him and exhaled, drying my son's wet face with the undampened hem of the rag. "If you give me a minute, I can try to get him back to sleep, and we'll find somewhere else to park."

"I can't do that, sorry," he said.

"Why?"

"Because I was raised better than that." He opened my door, reaching in to shut the window before he offered me his hand.

"I don't need your…"

"Yeah, you do. So does your baby." When I only stared at his offered hand, the man dropped his shoulders, like he was surprised I didn't hurry to do as he commanded. But he didn't lose his smile or let the harsh tone he used earlier return. "It's Christmas Eve. My parents own the best restaurant in this town, your baby is hungry, and you look like you haven't had a decent meal in months. And…I'm freezing my balls off standing out here talking to you. So, please, for the sake of the holiday…and my manhood, come inside."

I'd had worse offers. I'd had better, but he wasn't wrong. No one had asked me to dinner and certainly not with my kid. Ever. Besides, I couldn't be responsible for damage to this man's manhood. That would be a crime against all women everywhere.

"Okay," I told him, grabbing the bag before I moved myself and Mateo out of the car. "Thanks."

"Don't thank me yet."

"Why not?" I asked, some of that worry returning.

The man smiled, ushering me across the street. "Because you're about to witness a Carelli Christmas. You might prefer freezing in your car to my crazy family."

SMOKE

A few months back, Mickey Finney made threats, veiled ones, but still threats. The idling car across the street from the restaurant seemed suspicious. So, imagine my shock when it wasn't one of my enemies less-than-subtle kiss-asses, but a tired-looking woman with her head over the steering wheel and a screaming baby in her back seat.

She was tiny, waist that didn't give away the fact that she'd squeezed out a kid. Her skin was a smooth light brown, those beautiful Latina features set in a face without a line on it. I was sure she was still young, but the world-weary look in her eyes told me she was no child.

The woman walked ahead of me, her arms around that baby with the massive black eyes, his hands buried in the front of the dingy uniform she wore. Couldn't blame the kid. She had plenty up top I wouldn't mind playing with myself.

Shit.

I winced, blinking away the stupid thought at the imagined flash of my father's glare, accusing me of being a prick for checking out a nursing mother's rack. Couldn't be helped. I had a pulse, and this one was pretty.

"You got a man?" I asked her, leading her toward the restaurant, holding up my hand in apology when she shot me a frown. Pretty and a lot of fire. Couldn't say I hated that. "No offense meant. Just wanted to know if there was someone I should call or have one of my boys pick up," I said, steering her away from a slick spot of ice near a snow-covered drain. I *was* a nosy fuck, but I was about to bring her around my people. I had to know who I was dealing with. "I'm just saying, if it were me and I had a woman and a kid stranded in a place they clearly didn't know, and some asshole comes around bringing them in from the cold, I'd want a heads-up."

She relaxed, but only enough to ask a question. "You wouldn't say thank you first?"

"First," I said, shaking my head, "I'd wanna know his angle."

"And when you knew it?" she asked.

She paused in front of the door when I grabbed the handle, one black eyebrow lifted like she couldn't move until I gave her a good answer. So, I did my best. "If I like his angle, then I thank him. If I don't, I teach the fucker a lesson."

The eyebrow lowered, and there was

no frown lingering on her face. I got that maybe she liked what I had to say. Maybe she liked the little possessive streak I had when it came to what I saw as mine. But the truth was, I made sure no woman was ever mine for long.

"You know, you shouldn't curse so much around babies," she told me.

That made me laugh, an honest burst of amusement I hadn't felt in years. "You think he knows what I mean when I call someone a fucker?"

She grinned, glancing down at the boy in her arms. "I think he knows more than any of us realize."

"All right then, Miss…whoever the hell you are. I promise not to curse around your kid…whoever the hell *he* is."

"Fine," she said, smiling for the first time since I'd gotten a good look at her.

One glance at that pretty smile had me thinking she should do that a hell of a lot more.

CHELLE BLISS & EDEN BUTLER

She moved her hair behind her ear, slipping her gaze to the door where I had my fingers curled around the handle. "You gonna open it, Mr…whoever *you* are?"

"Smoke," I told her, waiting for the laugh I knew would come. Most women who didn't know me, who knew nothing about me *or* my family, tended to laugh when they heard my name. I hadn't met many of those, but it'd happened a time or two. "Smoke Carelli."

The name didn't make her frown, but there was obvious recognition in her features. "I'm guessing your mama didn't name you Smoke."

I shook my head. There wasn't time for the long story of where I got that name. Besides, it was cold as hell out here.

She nodded again. "Okay, fine then. Smoke." She stretched out a hand, curling her sleepy-looking baby closer to her chest as she offered it to me. "I'm Maggie

Ramirez, and this—" she moved the kid, his head wobbling against her collarbone before he blinked up at me "—is my boy, Mateo."

"Maggie and Mateo…Ramirez?" It was a question with a lot of meaning. If she had no man and the kid had her name, then there was no man at all and she was on her own. That explained the shitty uniform and shittier car.

"Yes," she said, her voice quiet, but her chin lifted. "I don't have a husband, and Mateo's only got me."

"Well, come on, Maggie." I opened the door, exhaling as the warmth from inside the restaurant began to chip away at the tightness in my fingers. "Tonight, you've both got a big family that's gonna get all in your business."

"Really, that's sweet, but I just need to borrow a phone to call my *tía*." We moved through the lobby and were immediately drawn into a small crowd. My uncle

Vinnie and cousin Leo were arguing about the Pats' chances at the Super Bowl. Maggie didn't need to hear that shit.

"Where is she?" I asked, holding her out of the way of a server who charged from the kitchen with a tray of shots.

"In the city."

I nodded for her to follow me behind the waiter but stopped when she tugged on my arm. "What's the problem?"

"You're sweet, but all of this…" She waved to the small crowd of my relatives and friends who stopped in the middle of their conversations to stare at us. "This is a little overwhelming. I don't belong here. This is a family dinner, and I'm a stranger to them. And my baby…"

"Will get the attention of every woman in the room." I stepped closer, hoping my voice didn't have the same bossy tone my kid sister Antonia swore I could never get rid of. "It's Christmas Eve, and you're on your own."

She opened her mouth to argue but closed it when I touched her arm.

"Call your *tía*, tell her what's going on, but there's no way you will get anywhere in this shit." Maggie followed the small jerk of my chin when I nodded it toward the window behind her.

In just the few minutes it took us to cross the street, the snow had fallen in sheets, so thick now that the sidewalks weren't visible.

"There's so many of them," she whispered, her eyes wide, gaze shooting around the crowd, those dark eyes getting bigger when someone laughed loudly and cackled behind me.

"Yeah. And they're a pain in the ass." I turned, glancing over my shoulder to nod at Mrs. Jonah, a perpetually horny widow who owned the bar five blocks over, as she tried to get Antonia and her ex Luca to kiss. Something the man promised me he'd never do again.

Luca glanced at me, shrugging, then distracted the old woman with a shot of vodka.

"But," I told Maggie, ignoring the look my sister was giving me and the one that followed from two of my aunts as I moved Maggie toward the kitchen, "you'll never meet nicer people."

"Dimitri?" I heard, trying like hell not to grunt when my mother's sister Maria called over the sound of laughter. "Who's that with you?"

"Incoming," I warned Maggie, turning to greet my aunt. "Maria, you look *bella*."

She waved me off, not bothering to acknowledge the kiss I planted on her cheek as she focused her attention on Maggie and the squirming bundle in her arms. "Look at you. Theresa!" Maria called, her attention on the swinging door leading to the bustling kitchen. "Come look at this beautiful baby." She brushed Mateo's face, making low, cooing sounds I'd never witnessed from the grumpy woman once in my life. "Ah, sweet *bambino*, he's so *bello*. How old?"

"Six months," Maggie said, her voice quiet. She didn't loosen her hold on the baby, especially not when my entitled aunt held open her arms, seeming like she expected Maggie to hand over her son without question.

"Maria, you can't go taking babies away from their mamas. She has no idea who you are," I told my aunt, not surprised when she waved me off.

Then my aunt covered her mouth, her attention shooting between me and Maggie, then down at the kid. "Oh my God! Does your mama *know?*"

"Know what?" For shit's sake, the woman was crazy. I let a grunt fly, not giving a solitary shit if I hurt the woman's feelings. "You serious?" I took a step back, eyes wide. "That's not…"

"Smoke isn't my son's father…" Maggie rushed out, like she was worried Maria would level her with a shitload of blame that wasn't hers.

"Of course, he isn't," I heard behind me, my stomach dropping when my mother approached. She was shorter and smaller than Maggie, but the look she gave her sister would have had even the meanest asshole pissing himself. "Maria, really. Now, who is this?" She faced Maggie, her attention landing on the nervous woman's face, holding her by the shoulders. "Oh, aren't you lovely? You know my son?"

"No, ma'am. I only just met him. I got lost." Maggie nodded to the window.

My mother looked to the left, her attention catching on the snow and the blanketed streets before she made out the busted Monte Carlo. "On your own? With this one?"

Maggie nodded, and my mother pressed a hand to her chest, like her heart had begun to race and her light touch would settle it.

"And my son brought you inside?" Ma asked, raising an eyebrow while glancing at me.

"More like…told me I *had* to come inside. But really, we can just sleep in the car. The heater works, and I'm sure the streets will be…"

"Oh no. No, I could never let you do that." Ma's grip on Maggie's shoulders tightened.

If I knew my mother, she was making plans she intended to see through, and Maggie wouldn't have much of a say in them. Once the woman started plotting, there wasn't much of a point in trying to stop her.

"So pretty, but how thin you are." She

snapped her fingers, as if something important had just occurred to her, and she turned to Maria. "Go fetch Antonia. Tell her to find something for…" She glanced at me, nodding to the woman standing in front of her.

"Maggie, and her son is Mateo. Maggie, this is my mother, Angelique."

"Ah," Ma said, turning back to her little sister. "Tell Antonia to find something for Maggie to wear for dinner."

Maria nodded, turning away, and I could see the argument surfacing on Maggie's tongue. Ma seemed to notice it too but cut the woman off by patting her hand and silencing her with a headshake.

"It would be rude to refuse. It's Christmas Eve, and you are alone. We will feed you and make you feel like one of us, but you must dress for dinner. It's proper, yes?" When Maggie nodded reluctantly, Mama smiled, her face brightening as she looked down at the baby. "Oh, he *is bello*. Can I hold him? It's been so long since I've held a baby."

"Sure," Maggie said, her gaze following my ma as she took the baby, making small, low sounds that only he seemed to understand.

"He is so strong and handsome. Reminds me of my Dimitri when he was little." She rubbed Mateo's cheek, her smile dimming as she moved her free hand away from the baby to smack me on the back of the head.

I jerked, not expecting the attack. "What the hell?" I said, rubbing the already throbbing injury.

"All my friends have grandbabies. I'll be dead before you make me a *nonna*, you selfish little…"

"Ma?" Antonia interrupted, nodding to Maggie. "Maria said you needed me?"

"Ugh, can she do nothing right?" Ma kissed Mateo's cheek, all evidence of her smacking me gone before she turned and placed the baby in my arms.

"What am I supposed to do with this?" I asked, holding the kid out in front of me by his waist.

"Hold him. Find something to feed him." She turned me around, taking the diaper bag from Maggie and ignoring the woman's complaints before she hooked the bag on my shoulder. "Maybe spending time with a *bambino* will warm you to the idea of giving your mama and papa grandbabies before they're dead in the grave."

"Ma, you're only sixty," Antonia said, holding up her hands when Mama glared at her.

I exchanged a look with my sister, nodding toward the kid, but she laughed at me, turning to follow our mother as she led Maggie toward the stairs to Antonia's old apartment.

"A little help here," I called to my sister, waving the fussing kid at her.

"Don't look at me. You're the oldest. You gotta go first."

"Let's get one thing straight…" I kept my eyes steady. No blinking. No squinting. This guy could sense a bluff. He could smell fear. "I don't like you."

The gurgle thing again. He'd been doing that shit for half an hour. Maria said they did that when they were teething, but I knew dick about all this shit. I only knew the little shit just ruined a $1500 suit, and there wasn't a damn person here who seemed willing to take him off my hands.

Not even my own men.

"Mr. Carelli, I'm sorry. Your mother left strict instructions…" Dino had admitted when Mateo puked all over my jacket and I told the man to take the kid to one of my aunts or cousins so I could clean myself up. "We aren't to let anyone but you hold that baby."

"My mother paying you now?" I asked, glaring at him.

Dino had frowned, shuffling his feet. "No, sir, of course not, but she's... Well, I gotta say, between the two of you, I'd rather not be on *her* shit list."

So, there I was, staring down a six-month-old, without my fucking jacket, sleeves rolled up to my elbows. I had a bowlful of mashed bananas Betty, the head chef, had whipped up for the kid in my hand, and I was glaring at the boy.

"You don't even have to chew it." The kid slobbered, using his tongue and lips to release a spray of saliva. He laughed, a deep, surprised noise catching in him as he tried the sound again.

The little asshole did it again, spraying

banana across my cheek. I threw the bowl onto the table beside me, grabbing a towel to wipe my face clean. Mateo wasn't concerned with anything but the new sound he seemed to have discovered, releasing one spit bubble after another over and over again.

Then, he laughed.

"Yeah, kid. You're fucking hilarious." I tossed the rag on the table, and I miscalculated my landing. The thing fell right across the baby's face, covering it completely. "Shit. Sorry," I said, jerking the towel off his face.

For some reason, the kid found the sudden appearance of my face fucking hysterical. The laughter returned, those giant black eyes disappearing as he cackled and giggled and, fuck me, I couldn't help it, that little shit had me laughing too. It was infectious, that small, wild laugh, along with those deep-set dimples.

He only quieted when a loud hiccup unsettled him, and the smile disappeared from his face, like he had no clue what the hell that noise was that left his throat. Then, the scared, worried frown started up, and I grabbed him before the water-works kicked in.

"You're good," I told him, standing with him, copying the same rocking motion I'd seen Maggie do earlier. It seemed to work, and Mateo calmed, reaching up to grab hold of my collar until he loosened the chain around my neck.

The crucifix was old, and he seemed fascinated by the small figure on the cross, so I didn't take it from him. Instead, I just watched the boy, wondering what kind of asshole would let his woman and his boy out on their own to fend for themselves.

Mateo shifted his gaze, pulling his attention from the crucifix to look up at me, his smile returning when he caught me watching him. Like he knew what a liar I was when I said I didn't like his tiny ass.

"What?" I asked him, adjusting the boy as I moved to the window along the back of the kitchen. The small staff continued to plate the food into serving dishes as I brought the baby to a quieter section, away from the ovens and the loud noise of conversation coming from the dining room.

The kid still watched me.

"You know," I explained, like a baby could understand a thing I said, "you're lucky you're almost as cute as your mama, kid. Otherwise, I wouldn't bother."

He gurgled again, his grin widening when I shook my head at him. The dimples were deeper now, and his eyes almost disappeared when he flashed a toothless smile.

"Don't get ideas. Those dimples don't do shit for me."

"Dimitri," Antonia called from the

CHELLE BLISS & EDEN BUTLER

door, and I turned, moving my chin to ac-knowledge her. "They're ready. Bring the baby."

The servers carried the food from the kitchen, and Mateo's gaze moved with each tray of pasta, ham, and fish as we walked toward the dining room. Ma had had the busboys position all the tables edge-to-edge, making one long table down the length of the entire restaurant.

"Here," Antonia said, reaching for Mateo when we made it to the table. "I'll take him."

For some reason, I felt possessive over someone who wasn't my family. "Fuck off," I told her, smiling when she flipped me the bird.

She shook her head, muttering some-thing I knew she'd never say if Pop were around.

"And stay the hell away from Luca."

Antonia laughed, looking across the table for the man in question. When she

38

caught his attention, she nodded him over, motioning to the empty seat next to the one she'd chosen.

Luca was too much of a chickenshit to look at me before he sat. I thought of calling him out, but my ma chose that precise moment to appear, pulling a very different-looking Maggie behind her.

And then, I didn't give a shit about Luca and Antonia, drooling babies, or Christmas Eve dinner.

She was wearing a fitted red dress I remember calling indecent when Antonia wore it in public. But on Maggie, it was perfect—it fit her luscious, full curves, moving when she did. Ending mid-thigh, the dress gave a tease that there was so much more to the woman than a hard worker and a tired single mother.

I lifted the baby when he wiggled in my arms. "Sorry, kid," I told him, unable to keep my attention from Maggie as she walked toward me. "She's got you beat."

Then I handed the boy over to Antonia, not waiting to see if she wanted him still or not, before I met Maggie by an empty chair, pulling it out for her.

I liked the way her pretty face brightened and how she watched my hand on the back of the chair.

"Um...*gracias*," she said, sitting straight, looking more elegant than uncomfortable. She split her attention between Mateo, who was happily bubbling spit at Antonia and Luca, before she looked me over.

"You look...beautiful," I told her, leaning closer.

"Oh. Um..." That blush grew redder, and this time, Maggie smiled. "Thanks, Smoke."

There was still a small look of hesitation on her face, along with a hint of worry. I knew that look. I'd seen it before. But I'd never been the one to put it on a woman's face.

Maggie went perfectly still when I stretched my arm around the back of her chair, angling closer. She smelled like the sweetest perfume. Her mouth was full and pink, her skin looked soft and warm, and I was not thinking of any woman but the one inches from me now.

"I don't pay compliments," I told her. "When I give them, I mean them. And right now, I fucking mean it."

"So…you're not…"

"Angling?"

"Yeah," she said, her face relaxing, "that."

"No, I'm not angling." I leaned back but kept my hand on her chair. "Not before dinner anyway."

"Friends," my mother said, pulling my attention from the sweet smile on Maggie's face. "Welcome, welcome! We're so happy you're here with us…"

My ma was filling in for my father, who was off running an errand he wouldn't tell anyone about, which pissed me off, but now I was too distracted by Maggie to let it bother me anymore.

Ma repeated the same spiel Pop liked to make every year, and it was always good. Welcome everyone, thank them for coming, say a prayer, and then we'd eat.

But tonight, as my mother spoke of family and friends, old and new, my attention wasn't on her words or the familiar faces readying to celebrate. It wasn't even on the smirk on my beautiful mother's face as she paused in her speech to watch Maggie and me.

At that moment, my mind was on one thing and one thing only—giving Maggie and Mateo the best Christmas they'd ever had.

A nod of my head, a text to Dino and the plan was set in motion.

MAGGIE

Smoke Carelli was a dangerous man. I knew that the second he tapped on my window and our gazes locked.

It was in his eyes—those dark, rich eyes of his that could cut right through you. Hard as steel when he had you at a distance. In a split second, they shifted to warm and sweet when he had his guard down, which I suspected didn't happen a lot.

But as I walked into the dining room not ten minutes ago, spotted Smoke holding Mateo, and saw that kind, protective look in his eyes, something inside me melted.

Smoke was dangerous all right, but I was the one at the greatest risk. It wouldn't be hard for me to fall completely for that beautiful man.

Mateo hadn't had many men watch over him, not since Alejandro chose lines of white powder and a dripping, wet needle over his family.

For some reason, my son had taken to Smoke like he knew the man wasn't the brooding threat I suspected him to be outside on the snowy sidewalk.

"Maggie, eat," I heard from across the table. I forced a smile on my face when Smoke's sister Antonia waved her glass at my still-full plate. "If you don't, Mama or Maria will be by to fill it again."

"I couldn't eat another bite." My stomach was so full, and I'd spent the past twenty minutes pushing the delicious food around, trying to make it look like I'd eaten more.

It had taken everything in me to try to finish the plate the server set in front of me, then Smoke's mama directed the woman to give me more before I'd finished half of what I'd already been served.

"Better not say that too loud," Dario, Smoke's brother, said, leaning on his elbow next to me. He sat on my right with Smoke on my left. My senses were on overload with the attention both men were giving me. "Mama will run down here to spoon-feed you if she thinks you're too skinny."

"She hasn't left you alone much," I remarked, nodding toward their mother as she moved back toward our end of the table.

"Dario, my love," Mrs. Carelli said, resting her hands on her son's shoulders. "Did you get enough? You should eat more. When I think of the food they made you eat..." She squeezed her eyes tight like the ideas she had about Dario's five-year stint in Riker's was a nightmare she wouldn't allow herself to think about on Christmas Eve.

"Mama, I got enough," he told her. "I promise." Dario grabbed his mother's hand, squeezing it before he winked at me and threw me under the bus. "But Maggie doesn't look like she's going to finish this plate."

"What?" Mrs. Carelli jerked her attention to my face, then her gaze dropped to my filled plate. "You don't like it?"

"Mama," Smoke said, stretching his arm over the back of my chair again. "Dario is starting shit. That's Maggie's second plate, and you keep trying to feed her."

"She's a nursing mother—"

"Mrs. Carelli," I tried, worried I'd offended her, making sure I leveled a quick glare at Dario before I turned to look at her fully. "Honestly, it's all so delicious…"

"Mama, she ate plenty," Dario said, shrugging with a half apology I wasn't sure I bought. "I was just messing with her. You know…it's been a long time since I've been around a pretty girl."

Instantly, my face heated and the irritation at his teasing vanished. Like his brother, Dario was handsome, tall, maybe a little less refined. Definitely rougher around the edges, but I'd been around enough people who'd served time to know that was what happened when you went away.

Sometimes, it made them awkward. Still other times, it made them very out of practice, like Dario was now. He seemed happy to be with his family, but it had taken four drinks for him to get there.

Now, he was comfortable enough to flirt, and I couldn't say I hated it. Couldn't

CHELLE BLISS & EDEN BUTLER

say I hated Smoke's reaction to his brother's mild flirting either.

"Too long," Smoke said, leaning forward to glare at his brother. "Why don't you try to find another one?" He nodded down the table, motioning to a group of women with their heads together as they looked down the table at Dario and Smoke. "Seems like they're more interested."

"Why?" Dario asked, holding his glass in his hands, the grip loosening as he moved closer. "You afraid of a little competition?"

Oh. My. God.

"Not even if there was any. Which there isn't."

"You sure about that, big brother?"

Smoke laughed, his features hard. "Bring it on, asshole."

I blinked, shocked by their words.

"*Basta!*" I heard Mrs. Carelli say, then frowned as both Dario and Smoke flinched, cupping their ears. "On Christmas Eve? *Madonna Santa*!"

Across the table, Mateo cried and my breasts instantly ached. Luca, the handsome man sitting next to Antonia, looked a little helpless when my son fussed again, shifting him from one side of his large chest to the other before my baby started crying harder. I pushed back from the table, excusing myself from Mrs. Carelli and her two sons.

"I didn't know what to do…" Luca said, standing to give the baby to me, but he stopped when I smiled at him, waving off his apology.

"He's teething," I told him, taking Mateo, who calmed when I laid him against my chest. "Nothing is going to make him happy right now."

"Can we get you…" Antonia tried, but I shook my head.

"No, but thank you. I'll just walk him around a bit."

*S*now completely covered the streets now. From the large bay window on the other side of the restaurant, I could make out the frosted glass of the storefronts and the frozen leaves on the limbs nearly touching the gazebo in the town square.

My car was almost hidden under several feet of snow, and four men bundled in parkas and thick gloves had begun to shovel the streets, clearing a path on the sidewalk.

This was a weird little place. An hour from the city, Cuoricino felt like it was a million miles away. Like somewhere stuck in time, where people cared about their neighbors, hosted huge dinners, shoveled snow and, apparently, took in lost strangers from the cold.

Mateo whimpered, and I looked down at the soft features of his perfect face. It still felt terrifying to me how much I loved him. How scared I was sometimes to be the only person in the world he depended on.

And here we were, standing in a strange place, taken in by friendly people who have cared more for us than our own family.

"Maggie?" The deep, rich voice twisted something inside me. Something I hadn't felt for over a year, growing wilder and hotter as he sat next to me all night.

"Hmm?" I said, not turning to face Smoke.

"You good?" He came closer and that wild, hot sensation lowered, his scent filling my senses.

I nodded, not trusting myself to sound calm if I answered him.

He was behind me. Not touching. The heat from his body like a tease. Like a promise that only made the needful, long-forgotten sensation spark and move until I could recognize it for what it was.

Lust.

"And the baby?"

I looked down at Mateo, his soft, easy snores pulling a grin from me.

Smoke reached for my son's face, smoothing a finger over his forehead. "He'll be a heartbreaker."

"Not if I can help it," I said, looking back out the window.

"No," Smoke said, standing against the window, his back on the glass as he watched me. "I can't see him getting away with shit. Not with a woman like you raising him."

He didn't know me.

I didn't know him, but I got the feeling Smoke was a man who could read people well.

I was no idiot.

I'd heard the Carelli name.

He might not be *the* Carelli I'd heard

of, but I knew they were related. He looked a lot like his infamous mafia cousin Johnny.

"And what kind of woman do you think I am?"

He pushed off the window, standing right in front of me. If I weren't holding Mateo, there'd be only inches separating us.

"What a loaded fucking question."

I didn't react, like I was sure he expected. From what I'd seen of him, Smoke liked reactions. He liked responses. I gave him nothing.

The strategy worked, and the man continued. "All right then, Miss Ramirez…" He looked at my face, his fingers following as he brushed the hair from my eyes. "I think you're beautiful." Smoke inched closer, his fingers slipping down my face, to my neck, to tickle the slope of my throat. "I think you're strong and smart." He nuzzled my face.

I closed my eyes, taking in the sensation of the emerging scruff on his face and how it rubbed against my cheek when he leaned down to whisper in my ear.

"I think I wanted to bash my kid brother's face in when he flirted with you, and I love him more than anything."

"Smoke," I whispered, pressing closer to him, forgetting for just a second that there was a baby, *my* baby, in my arms.

"I think," he continued, moving back to look me in the eyes, "that the streets are dangerous to drive. You and Mateo will stay with me, and I'll give you a happy Christmas."

"I couldn't. You've already been too kind." A thought occurred to me, and I took a step back, wondering what he wanted from me, debating whether that would be such a bad thing.

He was so tempting, and God, did I want him.

"Don't think you owe me a thing," he

said as his attention slipped to the front of the building to a crowd of people laughing. "I have plenty of room. A bed for Mateo and you can take my room. I have a pullout I can crash on. But if you want…" Smoke licked his lips, moving his hand to my face to lift it up.

I thought he might kiss me, and I held my breath, waiting.

He angled my chin and moved closer, his full, wet lips glistening from the overhead light, but he stopped before he moved any closer. "If you want…you don't have to sleep alone."

He walked away, leaving me with my baby and the absolute belief that no one I had ever met was more dangerous than Smoke Carelli.

SMOKE

I didn't like being lied to.

Hit me. Steal from me, maybe.

But lie to me, and I got fucking offended.

Especially, when you promised not to do something, and two hours later, you did the very damn thing you gave your word you wouldn't do.

Like touch my little sister.

To be fair, she was a grown woman.

I got that.

I wasn't her keeper.

Antonia had had plenty of men in her

bed. Granted, I didn't want to know shit about that, and yeah, maybe I'd facilitated a few background checks and had a few conversations with assholes I knew were fucking my sister over. But this was different.

Luca DeRosa gave me his word to stay clear of Antonia, shaking my hand on it, then wormed his way into a family dinner, and sat right next to her all damn night.

Then I stepped away for ten damn minutes and they disappeared. Alone. Together.

"You didn't see where Antonia and Luca went?" I asked Dario, who clearly wasn't sober enough to get over being pissed at me. When he only shook his head, I grabbed his glass from him, pushing him back in his chair with one hand before he could stand. "Did you hear me?"

"Nope. Not my business."

"Our sister is not your business?" I asked him, tilting my head to look down at him. I handed off his glass to Dino when he approached my side.

"You do your own time, man. Let her be."

"Do your own…hey, asshole," I told him, kneeling down to his level. Dario was lit out of his skull. "You aren't in prison anymore."

He blinked at me, and it took him three full seconds before the dots seemed to connect.

"Yeah, you with me?"

Dario nodded, rubbing his eyes.

"Antonia?"

"Where's that girl? Maggie?"

I grunted, giving up, but still glanced down the table to where Maggie sat with my cousin Ricardo and his husband, David. Ma and Maria were arguing over who got to hold Mateo, and I tossed Maggie a smile when she looked up at me, hoping she knew I was serious about the offer I made.

She was wound tight. Probably hadn't let herself go since she got pregnant. A woman like that being closed off, holding back and keeping herself alone?

She needed to let go a little.

"Dino," I said, nodding my man over. "You see my sister?"

"Yes sir," he said, placing Dario's glass on the tray of a passing server. "'Bout a half hour ago she and that Luca fella went upstairs."

A small ache started to pinch at the base of my skull, but I ignored it, nodding to Dino. "I gotta handle something. Keep my brother away from Maggie, and get someone to grab him some coffee. I don't want my father to come back and see him like this."

"Yes, sir. I'm on it."

By the time I made it to the stairs and cleared the first five steps, Antonia was coming down. Her hands were in her hair as Luca followed behind her with a smug, satisfied grin on his face as he adjusted his tie.

They both stopped when they saw me.

"Shit," Antonia said, then quickly recovered. "What?" She was immediately defiant, unapologetic, and tried to pretend not to be bothered by the look I gave her. But Antonia never really had been able to shake the need to make her family happy. She wanted everyone to be proud of her. It was a remnant of the troublemaker she was as a teenager. The little shit had caused our parents more tears than the three of us boys combined, and as she got older, Antonia felt guilty about it. But my sister was stubborn. Prideful.

I didn't answer her. Instead, I took in a breath, hoping it would calm me, hoping there was enough Christmas spirit to keep me from knocking the shit out of Luca DeRosa.

One slip of my gaze to his collar, to the smudge the exact color of my little sister's lipstick, and I realized the Grinch had taken me over. "Antonia," I said, looking directly at Luca, "excuse us for a second."

"No," she tried, her voice whiny, high. She looked between us like she expected the frown on her face to keep the glares from passing between me and the man she can't seem to keep out of her system. "Brother, I'm thirty years old, you have no right to…"

One jerk of my eyes to her, leveling the same threatening stare I reserved for anyone who got between me and my business, and my sister went quiet.

"It's okay, Toni," Luca said. "It's just business."

She touched his hand, squeezing his fingers. She turned to me, her features tight as she muttered, "Don't you dare ruin this for me," and left the stairs.

I watched her, making sure she was gone before I opened my mouth. "You got that wrong," I said, nodding to Uncle Vinnie as he moved past the stairwell and onto the patio. "You and me, DeRosa, we got no business to discuss."

"Smoke…"

"Merry fucking Christmas," I said and walked away from the staircase, heading back into the dining area, ignoring my sister as she brushed past me.

Like I said, I don't like liars.

❋

I hadn't had a cigarette in ten years.

Not once.

But tonight, I thought I might need one.

Antonia wasn't speaking to me. Dario was sober now and pissed at me about that shit too. Maggie was stuck between my mama and Maria telling her the best way to wean a baby without having her tits sag—a conversation I didn't want to hear. By the look on her face, she was clearly mortified they were having the talk in the middle of the fourth course of Christmas Eve dinner.

I moved outside onto the patio, finding Dino near the parking lot, debating whether or not to bum a smoke from him. It was stupid to even consider it.

Ten years was a long time, and even being around the smell of smoke irritated me most days. But my nerves were bad and getting worse the longer the night wore on.

"Everything okay, boss?" my man asked, waving his hand to keep the smoke away from me as he made for the ashtray.

"Finish your smoke, man. I just needed a break from that shit."

Dino looked at me, his head tilting to

the side, his eyes narrowed. "You want one?"

I waved a hand, but he still pulled out a pack of Marlboro Reds.

"You smoke that shit and your mama will have your balls," I heard, turning toward the sound of my father's voice.

"Pop," I greeted.

The smile on my face shook when I spotted my youngest brother Dante at our father's side. He'd been spending time with our cousins in White Plains since returning from Italy and even though I'd seen him a lot since he'd been back, I still wasn't used to how different he was.

Dante looked nothing like that scrawny shit my folks sent packing to Pistoia five years ago when Dario agreed to take the bid for the stupid shit Dante had done. Drug running, in Dario's bar. Pops had figured if Dario insisted on doing Dante's bid for him—pretty little thing he was would have never survived Riker's—

then the kid would have to learn his lesson.

Seems he had.

"We're all finally here. Our first Christmas together in years," Pop said, seeming to sense the tension.

"Yeah," I said, shaking off the small irritation I still felt at my kid brother. "Ma's happy everyone is home," I agreed with him, turning to nod inside the restaurant to where Dario leaned against the wall, his fingers wrapped around a mug of coffee.

Ignoring me, Dante headed inside, grinning when Ma and Antonia jumped from their seats to hug him, followed by several of the cousins and aunts.

Dario seemed to take everything in, watching all the affection Dante got—not nearly as warm a reception as he'd gotten when he'd returned from prison.

"Dario isn't going to let this shit go easy," I told my father.

"It's Christmas, son. Your brothers won't disappoint their mama on Christmas."

"Dario hasn't had a Christmas on the outside in five years, Pop. Whose fault is that?"

My father stared at me, his eyebrows shooting up. "His."

I opened my mouth, ready to argue, but his shaking head stopped me.

"No one asked him to take the blame, not even Dante. In fact, if I remember right, Dante wanted to go to the DA and make a confession, but Dario wouldn't have it."

"Still…"

"We all make choices, and we all have to deal with them." Pop turned, glancing at Dino when another of my men approached to speak to him. My father ignored them, shrugging off my business and employees as he headed for the door. "Now, if you don't mind, I want to see my wife and go inside to eat. It's fucking cold out here, and it's Christmas."

Pop disappeared inside, tearing off his coat as Mama approached, her face wide with a smile.

"What's the problem?" I said, frowning as another of my guys joined Dino and the other man who I now saw was Mike. Nodding to both, I slipped my hands into my pockets, frowning at the looks on their faces. "Speak."

"Mr. Carelli," Dino started, "Mike and Rickey say there's a problem with one of the business owners."

"Oh?" I walked forward, forgetting about the cold that had settled into my bones, my curiosity piqued. "Who is it?"

Mike motioned toward the edge of the patio. "The bakery across the street." He directed me across the patio and down some small steps until we could see a large van and a building lit up just across the way from my parents' restaurant.

Then in the distance, I could clearly make out a woman in a thick coat, her long red hair in a braid down the center of her back.

"So, what's the problem?" I asked, angling my head to get a better look at her.

She came into the light, holding a large box in her arms with a bag hanging from her elbow.

"She refuses to pay the protection fee."

The words hung in the air like the hot breath coming from my mouth. The Realtors jazzed it up as a community fee. Sometimes they said it was a town expenditure tax or a preservation fee, but it was always mandatory and stipulated in every mortgage agreement new tenants sign.

"Did I hear you right?" I said, turning to stare at my men.

That fee wasn't for me. It was for the town. It kept the dockworkers from losing our cargo and inspectors happy enough that our deliveries didn't get shipped to larger townships or bigger cities. It kept the town from being harassed by other families wanting to take over all those gray businesses I tried hard to keep out of our community.

So why the hell wouldn't she pay it?

"Yes, sir. Turns out she's got some fancy lawyer who argued the fees weren't legal because the taxes aren't part of the town charter and were never voted on."

"No shit, they weren't voted on…"

"Mr. Carelli," Dino said, stepping between Mike, Rickey, and me as I watched the woman come back to the van empty-handed. "I can go talk to her. Maybe make her understand how things are here. What we offer as far as our protection goes…"

She stopped near the back of the van, head turning like she knew we were watching her. My men looked away, worried, I guess, of getting caught. The red-

CHELLE BLISS & EDEN BUTLER

head lifted her head, one hand on her hip, like she was waiting for me to move or comment or do any damn thing but watch her.

"No," I finally told Dino, unable to keep the grin off my face. "It's Christmas. We've got time."

"Dimitri," I heard, turning to see my father waving me inside.

I nodded to him, tapping Dino once on the chest before I left my men. "You take care of that thing for the girl I asked you about earlier?" I asked Dino.

"Yes, sir," he said, nodding to Mike and Rickey. "They'll drop it off the second you text me that everyone's asleep.

"Good. Thanks. Have a good one."

I slipped inside, relieved as the rush of heat greeted me and on edge from the argument I could hear from my spot next to Maggie and Mateo.

"Sorry," I told her, touching her

shoulder when I sat. "Had to take care of something."

Mateo sat in his mother's lap, his big eyes getting wider as he watched Antonia and Dante bickering across the table.

"Are they…always like this?" Maggie asked, leaning closer to whisper in my ear. She smelled like wine, sweet, delicious, and a little like lilacs, making me want to nibble on her neck right here at this table with my idiot siblings irritating everyone.

"Always," I told her, grabbing Mateo's hand when he reached for my finger. "Antonia is protective of Dario. She's still pissed at Dante, but she loves him too." I grabbed a glass of wine, my finger still in the baby's death grip. "Even if he is an asshole."

Mateo giggled when Antonia threw part of her roll at Dante, and he retaliated by flinging a strawberry at her head, making her yelp.

Her face went red and blotchy until she screamed with a loud, *"Bafangu!"*

Not exactly something a kid should ever say around their parents, no matter how old they were, especially not around a crowd of people on Christmas Eve.

"Antonia Maria Carelli!" Mama shouted, slamming her fist onto the table. "Enough!"

My sister and Dante straightened, both instantly looking down at their plates as Pops stood, resting a hand on Mama's back. His expression shifted from a frown to a smile as he gazed around the room.

"I'm so happy my wife got to speak for me earlier, but I'd like to say something too…if you wouldn't mind?" Our family and friends clapped, their attention shifting instantly from my stupid siblings to our father. Next to me, Mateo reached, his small arms outstretched, and I took the hint, grabbing the kid to hold him in my arms.

"Okay," I told him, my voice in a whisper, "as long as you remember the dimples shit doesn't work on me."

He went for my crucifix again, and I let him, stretching an arm around the back of Maggie's chair. She leaned back, resting against my chest, her hand slipping onto my knee like it was habit, something I didn't think she meant to do.

It didn't bother me, didn't seem to bother her either at first. Then she glanced down, her eyebrows shooting up like she'd only just realized what she was doing.

Yeah, she wants it.

When she started to move away, I grabbed her hand, holding my fingers over hers to keep her there. "You're good," I told her, smiling when I spotted how her chest heaved the closer I leaned toward her. "I don't mind if you don't."

She looked up at me then as my father went on about his family, this town, and the importance of friendship and forgiveness. All I could think of were those big brown eyes and the touch of her hand as she stroked the inside of my thigh. Then Maggie bit her lip, those top teeth dragging along the wet skin.

And I realized for the first time that night, there was something I wanted for Christmas too.

MAGGIE

I was weightless.

Floating.

For the first time in over a year, it felt like there was nothing I had to worry about. There was nothing I had to think of except how it felt to sleep, relax, and just be.

Then I felt something soft, plush, comfortable, unlike anything I'd ever felt before. A cloud. A pillow. A mattress?

My eyes flew open as the weightlessness ended. I jerked upright, grabbing around me, my hands reaching, panic overtaking me. "Mateo? *Mijo*? Where are you?"

"Maggie. Shh…" Smoke. His arms. Strong, solid. "He's fine. I got you. He's asleep."

"Where?" I said, brushing the hair from my face. I was still in Antonia's dress, but the shoes were gone and so were the earrings. "Where's my son?"

"Here," he told me before holding my hand, leading me down a short hallway and into a bedroom, the door open wide.

There was a bed outfitted with a thick quilt pushed to the edge of the mattress. In the center was my son, on his back, his arms outstretched, surrounded by a ring of pillows Smoke seemed to have made for him.

"Yes," I said, laughing under my breath.

Men were clueless about babies but damn cute sometimes.

"You can hear him if he cries," he

told me, leading me back toward his room. "The place is old and solid, but the vents make it impossible to keep many secrets. If he cries, you'll know."

"You're the only one in the building?" I blinked with my mouth hanging open.

"My folks took Dario to their place, and the street sweepers got the snow cleared," he said, untucking his shirt. As I watched him, pressing my lips together, probably looking a little desperate, Smoke stopped, moving closer, but not close enough to touch me. "I'll take the pullout couch so you can rest in here." His tone was light, but the inflection was open-ended, like he wasn't sure if that was what he wanted to do. Like he was pretty sure that was not what I wanted him to do at all.

The shirt he wore was high-end, the sleeves rolled and still unwrinkled. It fit him like it was sewn onto him. This branch of the Carelli family tree may not be *the* Carelli family, but they certainly weren't poor.

Smoke's home was lush, his furnishings ornate and comfortable. There were no discount IKEA pieces in this place. No overstock purchases or last-season designs filling his closets. Like the dress I borrowed from his sister, everything was new and designer, with just a bit of overkill. But on Smoke, it didn't seem over the top.

It seemed pretty damn good.

He appeared to be waiting for me to do something. He didn't have to wait long. I'd gone a long time not touching anyone but myself.

I didn't love Smoke Carelli, but I did want him.

I needed him to touch me, and I wanted desperately to touch the fine lines of his taut, strong body. I wanted to taste the smooth slope of his thin waist and deep ridges that dipped past his navel.

"Smoke," I whispered, standing in front of him, taking his hand in mine.

He raised his eyebrows, a silent acknowledgment.

"I don't want to be in here alone."

He wet his lips, moving his teeth over his bottom one while he looked at me like he needed me to be clear. "You want me to sleep in here?"

"Not so much, no."

He moved close, curling one hand around my waist. "You want me to fuck you in here?"

I laughed, my mouth pulling up at one side. "Damn, *papi*, you have a filthy mouth."

"*Bellissima*, you're about to find out just how filthy my mouth is."

I was not ready for him.

Smoke wasn't slow and sweet. He was a man who took what he wanted, when he wanted it, and right then, it was me.

He pulled me to him, our bodies flush,

grabbing me by the waist just as his mouth landed on mine, kissing me hard.

Smoke filled my mouth. His greedy tongue dove in as he gripped his fingers first on my waist, then onto my ass, tugging me closer and closer.

I felt every inch of him getting harder —the straining tightness of his arms as he reached for me, the contours of his chest as I scratched my fingers over his pecs, and the long, insistent firmness of his thick cock as he pressed closer against me.

"Smoke. Closer. Please…" I told him, slipping a leg around his hip, moaning when he held me close.

Then, the smug asshole teased me, gripping my hair between his fingers as he held my head still. He looked down at me, holding my leg so he could grind against me, demonstrating how thick and swollen he was for me.

"You feel that?"

I nodded, shuddering each time he brushed against me.

Smoke grinned, his hold on me tightening. "You want that? You sure?"

"*Sí*... Yes... I want...*all* of that." God, I sounded like such a needy whore, but there was something about how Smoke was looking at me in a way that I didn't feel cheap.

"Good. That's good, baby." Smoke pulled my head toward him, taking my mouth again, devouring it, until I was breathless. Until I was shuddering from the command of his tongue and his control.

He moved us, lying me across the bed, his lips on my neck, greedy, anxious fingers working down the zipper at the back of the dress. As he pulled down the dress and uncovered my skin, he kissed across my body, along my collarbone. His mouth and tongue skated over my breasts, sucking on my nipples, nibbling down my ribs until he had me naked. Smoke had my legs in his hands and held me open, staring down at me when I reached across my belly to cover myself.

"Don't do that," he told me, pushing my hands away. "You're beautiful. Fucking delicious. So fucking sexy."

"I'm not…"

He wouldn't hear any reasons I might have had for disagreeing with him. Smoke ignored me completely and dipped between my legs, his mouth covering my pussy, tongue deep, licking, and sucking. I forgot instantly what I was saying or why I'd ever believed I could do without this for a single second.

"Oh God… God!"

He cupped my bottom, holding me against his mouth as I tangled my fingers in his hair, wanting him closer, needing him deeper. And when I thought I couldn't stand any more sensation, Smoke slipped his thumb inside me, working against my G-spot, his finger moving until I tightened around him and my orgasm crested. "Yes! Oh…yes!"

Smoke watched me, that sweet, slow grin turning into a full-on smile as my body relaxed and my heartbeat returned to normal. I reached for him, wanting to kiss him, needing more from him.

"Come here, *papi*," I said.

He listened, for once, leaning forward, tugging off his shirt, slipping out of his pants and shorts until all there was of him was that smooth olive skin and those glorious, lean muscles and his perfect, long cock.

He barely fit in my hand. The tip was wide but warm as I slipped it between my lips. Smoke moaned, leaning back on one arm to watch me move over him. His low humming moans were nearly as sexy as the feel of his dick inside my mouth.

"That's good, beautiful… *Fuck*, that's good…" He tangled his fingers in my hair again, guiding me. The low grunts were deeper now, and when I used more suction, that grunt became a moan before he pulled me off him. "Not too much," he told me, gaze on my mouth, before he kissed me, pushing me back onto the mattress. "That pretty mouth is too sweet. You're gonna make me come too fast, and I wanna be deep inside you when I do that."

Smoke kissed me again, rising to his knees, smoothing his hands over my breasts and down my stomach before he kissed the center of my chest. "So fucking beautiful." He placed one final kiss against my mouth before he reached for his bedside table and removed a condom, opening it with ease. Stroking himself, his gaze on my face, he smoothed it over his cock. "Lie back," he told me, crawling closer, positioning himself over me, "and spread yourself wide."

Smoke distracted me with a deep,

hard kiss. His tongue demanding, the suction drugging as he moved his hips and guided himself slowly inside.

It had been over a year since I'd had sex. No one had touched me since I found out I was pregnant…since Alejandro.

My body ached with each stinging touch of Smoke's cock moving inside. The ache was sweet. The heat scorching. Every thrust, every rock of his hips against mine, took away the memory of what I'd been missing for the past year.

"Maggie, you sweet fucking beauty… You're perfect wrapped around me… *Shit*…"

Smoke moved faster, holding on to my hip, looking down to watch the way we moved together, how he moved inside me. I loved the expression on his face. How we seemed to fascinate him. How we seemed to turn him on.

Then I tightened, loving the friction, remembering this sensation, wanting it harder, so I told him, "Go…go deeper…"

"Fuck yes…" he said, like he was relieved I didn't want him to hold back.

No more gentleness.

No more caution.

I wanted Smoke to give me everything he could.

"Open up, baby. Open wide."

I listened, spreading my legs, bringing my knees up. Smoke immediately responded, holding my inner thighs, grinding inside me, going so deep it was almost painful. He leaned forward, resting one palm on the pillow above my head, and he slowed his movements, making them deeper still, touching me further than anyone had before.

The sensation was new, overwhelming. I felt myself beginning to crest, the hum of an orgasm starting in the center of my body and working its way down.

Smoke moved faster, trying to catch

me like it was a race we were both trying to win, until I fell over the edge.

"Fuck!" I said, arching as I came.

"Shit," Smoke said, gripping the pillow, his forehead against mine, his breath heavy and labored until we both went perfectly still.

SMOKE

My parents taught me to give.

If you had plenty and someone was in need, you gave until that need was met.

It wasn't in their nature to be greedy. They may have started their lives in that gray area and left it, I may live there now, but that didn't mean we were selfish.

It meant we were smart.

Calculating.

Maggie had a need, and I hope like fuck I met it. From the way she lay boneless against me, naked and glorious, I got the impression I did.

Christ, was she hot.

She let go completely, released everything. Did a little giving of her own last night.

She didn't stir when I moved her onto the pillow, brushing back the hair from her smooth, pretty face. There was no expression on her features. No worry or fear like there'd been when I'd carried her in here before she'd asked me to stay.

The anxious way she'd jerked awake, automatically reaching for the kid, desperate to find him, twisted something inside me.

Hated seeing her like that.

That shit came from fear and terror, like she expected someone to swoop in and steal away with her boy.

Maggie had a secret.

She had worries, and I planned to find out where all that shit came from.

She might not ever be my woman—a man like me couldn't afford attachments like a woman or a kid—but she needed someone to have her back. That much, I could do.

The sheet fell from my waist when I slipped away from her. I tugged on my pajama bottoms, stretching as I headed for the living room. The snow was everywhere, sheets of it. The sun would melt some of it, but the frigid temps would keep most of it on the ground. The weather would keep us indoors and give me time to work on Maggie and those secrets of hers.

There was a small cry from the hallway, and I walked through the open door, closing it softly before I headed to the second bedroom. Mateo was on his stomach, doing some baby version of a push-up when I walked in. Mateo's mouth split into a huge grin when he spotted me, and those dimples made an automatic appearance.

"What? It's Christmas, so you think

I'll soften up? No way, kid." I reached for him, taking him in my arms, and the dimples got deeper. "Your mama is still cuter, and the dimples still aren't doing shit for me."

He reached for my necklace again and gripped it, his eyes brightening when I held him closer.

"You gotta be hungry and…" I felt his ass and flared my nostrils. I hadn't done this kind of shit since Antonia and Dante were babies. "Fine," I told him, moving to the foot of the bed to find the pack of diapers and wipes to change him. "Listen to me, kid. I got a certain reputation, you understand?"

He pulled on his foot, muttering gibberish that only he seemed to get.

"I can't have you telling everybody you got Smoke Carelli to wipe your ass. You get me?"

Mateo grinned, not fighting me as I changed him.

I pulled his leg back into the weird-looking PJs Maggie had him in. I was sure I missed a few buttons. I didn't have a clue what to do with a shitty diaper, so I left it wrapped up on the bed, and brought the kid with me into the kitchen.

"That," I told the kid, pointing to the tree and the gifts in the living room Dino and the boys laid out sometime last night, "is why you maintain a good rep. So your boys stay loyal and do good work."

"He's a little young for career advice."

I turned, catching sight of a sleepy-looking Maggie as she stepped out of the hallway and finished a yawn. "Nah. Just a little friendly guidance." Her eyes closed as she grinned to herself before she blinked, bringing her attention straight to me in the kitchen, holding her boy.

Fuck, she looked good, all rumpled from the bed, her cheeks pink and skin glowing, like all she needed was a good orgasm and a long night's sleep on a decent mattress.

She must have found my stash of Yankees gear because she was wearing an oversized jersey that buttoned up, the solid blue one I'd worn helping Antonia move.

It was a little frayed and had a missing button at the top, which was likely why Maggie picked it. She wasn't the type to be greedy about shit that belonged to other people.

The jersey fell to the middle of her thighs, and her thick, black hair waved around her shoulders, nearly touching her elbows as she stepped closer.

But it wasn't that sexy-as-hell, sleepy, sex kitten vibe she was pulling off that caught my attention. It was the way her eyes had gone all wide and glinting, how the lights from the lit tree twinkled against the moisture in those eyes as she stared at it.

"Smoke…"

Maggie didn't need me to tell her whose names were written on all the presents under the tree. She could make out for herself that my family didn't need a new crib or stroller. They didn't need a tricycle or giant-sized stuffed bears. None of them had a need for a year's supply of baby food or diapers or wipes or any of the shit Dino and the boys stacked around the tree, wrapped with red ribbons. Antonia had her own clothes. She didn't need the ones wrapped up for Maggie or the coat and boots Ma sent up late last night along with jewelry and bags she'd never worn or used even once.

"Merry Christmas, beautiful," I told Maggie, taking her hand when it looked like she wasn't gonna move.

I expected a thank you.

Maybe a smile.

It was Christmas after all.

Before last night, I doubted Maggie

had shit in the way of hope of a good holiday for her boy.

But I didn't expect her to stop me just as we came to the tree.

I didn't expect her to pull her hand from my hold and take the baby.

"Maggie?" I asked when she shook her head.

Her eyes welled with tears again before she dropped her head, clinging to the baby like he was gonna give her any kind of comfort.

"Why the fuck would you do something like this?" she asked.

MAGGIE

I couldn't help my tone.

The words were harsh.

They bit, I knew that, and I sounded ungrateful.

Mateo didn't offer much protection from Smoke. He couldn't hide my face from the man when he stood in front of me.

There was a frown hardening his features, making him look like the scary gangster knocking his gun against my car window last night.

I tried not to let that look intimidate me, but it was damn hard.

"Mind explaining the problem?" Smoke sounded pissed, but under that irritation was a little offense, something I expected.

Something I understood.

He was only trying to help.

I turned my face, rubbing my wet cheeks against the back of my hand before I spoke. "This…all of this is too much. I couldn't possibly…" The words got twisted in my throat, stuck there behind all the ways I wanted to say thank you to him for how good he'd treated me. Despite the *loco* arguing and the ridiculous amounts of food they expected me to eat, they were funny and kind.

And Smoke… Jesus…he was a good man.

He was too good for me.

"When the snow clears," I told him, my face dry before I looked up at him,

"I'm going to take Mateo, and we'll never see you or your family again."

Smoke flinched, like he hadn't expected me to be honest or brutal, but I'd always believed it was better to rip off the Band-Aid quickly rather than to tear it off inch by inch. The pain eased faster that way.

"You are good people. You are kind, but you are not for me…for us. The gifts are too much. Too grand. Too big for our small place, for my small, busted car. Too…" I sighed, unable to finish my explanation. Like Smoke, everything was thoughtful, decadent, and beyond my means. "We will walk away with…grateful hearts for how generous you all have been…"

Smoke lifted one eyebrow, his gaze shooting to my chest, then lower, as though he thought I should remember that his generosity went well beyond dinner with his family. How could I forget? He was the best sex of my damn life.

"But… Smoke, we *will* still walk away."

There was a flash of something I couldn't place in his expression—anger? Irritation? Defiance? Whatever it was, Smoke kept it to himself. He didn't argue with me. He didn't debate. Instead, he squinted, his jaw clenching like it took effort not to speak before he exhaled, walking into the kitchen to take out the fixings for hot chocolate—the milk and cocoa, the whipped cream and marshmallows, glancing long enough to nod to his sofa, offering me a spot as he made quick work of his task.

Jesus, this man was bossy. But my breasts began to ache and Mateo rubbed his face over my chest, so I sat, letting him nurse while the beautiful, dangerous man made cocoa.

The Christmas tree was massive, likely

ten feet, but still didn't come close to reaching the fifteen-foot ceilings of Smoke's apartment. Everything in this place was industrial but modern, with masculine touches and old-world hints placed sparsely along the walls in the brightly colored artwork and rich, lush pillows and rugs.

The Christmas décor was detailed and complemented the style of the place along with the hues of red, gold, and green in the tree. There was garland draped around the windows and along the freestanding kitchen island and over the wall-length bookcase against the entry wall.

Under the tree were dozens of presents. I spotted Mateo's name on most, but a few smaller ones and some gift bags had my name written in boxy square letters on the tags.

I felt the same unworthy sensation welling inside me. The inclination to bolt returned, but then I reminded myself that my clothes were downstairs in the restaurant, likely guarded by Mrs. Carelli, who made me promise to eat a family lunch with them before I left for the city.

"So," Smoke said, placing a large mug of cocoa in front of me. The top was covered in whipped cream and sprinkled with chocolate powder. "Explain this nonsense to me."

"It's not nonsense," I tried, nodding a thanks for my cocoa. "It's just the way things are."

Smoke held his mug in one hand but didn't drink from it. There was no whipped cream on his, and from the smell wafting over the rim, I suspected there was a healthy shot of bourbon inside it.

"My parents spent the first ten years of their marriage in a one-bedroom, fifth-floor walk-up because Pop refused to work any job for his brother." He leaned back, resting his leg on his knee. "You know about my uncle and cousin?"

I nodded but didn't dare ask any of the hundreds of questions I had about the Carelli family. It wasn't important right now.

Smoke grinned, tightening his eyes after he took a sip of his cocoa. "Then you know it took balls for my pop to turn his brother down." Smoke took another sip, but this one didn't make him wince. "Everything my parents have, they earned, and while not all of their businesses were always one hundred percent legal, they were always fair. No one went hungry because of them, and they always gave back. The point is, what we have now is a blessing. It isn't the way things have always been. So, you'll have to do better than 'all of this is too much,' because that shit doesn't make a lot of sense to me."

"Why?"

Smoke relaxed against his seat, moving his cup to the table next to him. "I make no judgments. God knows, I got no right to criticize how anyone lives their life." He licked his lips. It seemed like he had to think about what he could say without insulting me. "You're a good mother and a sweet, caring woman. But you show up wearing a dingy uniform, shoes with the soles frayed and thin, driving the oldest fucking Monte Carlo I've ever seen in the world, a car that's so cold you had to wrap your baby up in two quilts to keep him warm."

"Yes?" I said, turning my head to the side, challenging him with a glare. "What of it?"

"Your will is great, but your resources are shit. From where I'm sitting, there is no 'too much' for you because you have nothing. You'll continue to have nothing if you don't swallow your pride and let someone help you."

"I don't need anything from…"

"Maybe not," he said, leaning forward to rest his elbows on his knees. "But your kid does, doesn't he?" Smoke watched me.

I curled Mateo closer, cradling him as he nursed and clung to the shirt I was wearing.

The man nodded, motioning to my son, his gaze shooting over to his cup when he grabbed it. "He's a sweet kid. He'll make you proud. I'm guessing that didn't come from the man who made him."

"No," I said, my face going warm when I had a flash of Alejandro standing in the middle of our apartment, his hands shaking as he tore through the contents of my purse, trying to find where I'd put the last of the cash we had left.

I knew then, that was it. I'd told him about the pregnancy test that morning, and he hadn't even reacted.

"No," I said again. "This baby is mine. He's all mine."

"So, the father is…"

"Not going to be in his life."

Smoke nodded but didn't look away. The same knowing, measure-you-up look returned to his features, and I understood he wanted more information. He'd been good to us. I owed him my gratitude, maybe a little trust, but not everything.

"I'd rather my baby be the son of a poor woman than one of a drug addict."

"How about the kid whose mom makes enough at her new gig that he doesn't have to be either?"

Smoke met my gaze, his mouth re-laxed before it moved into a smile.

But I was hesitant.

I didn't need charity.

I didn't do handouts.

"I can literally hear the 'no' working its way up your throat. Before you turn me down and start in with all the bullshit excuses, let me remind you, this town is closer to your aunt than whatever shithole place you're from. My folks own a building two blocks over with income-based rent and affordable day care, but you won't need it for long." He leaned back, stretching his long legs out in front of him. "My parents like to hire servers with goals. They like to see people advance. You want to work for them, you gotta have a game plan. You don't have one yet, but they can help you figure that out."

"I...I have a degree. I just... No one wanted to hire a pregnant dance major who hadn't been in a company in three years because her asshole boyfriend convinced her being a ballerina wasn't a viable career option for a CEO's wife."

"Prick," he said, his expression tight like if he could find Alejandro right now, he'd smash his face in. Smoke wouldn't be the only one.

"I'm the one who listened to him," I said, waving him off. "You think your parents would really consider…"

"Who do you think told me to ask you?" Smoke laughed, moving to my side when Mateo stopped suckling and began to snore. "My ma had plans for you and the kid inside of a half hour of meeting you. If you're not careful, she'll have you married off to a cousin or…" He frowned, looking away like he wasn't sure he wanted to finish that sentence.

Smoke followed my hand when I moved it to his thigh and leaned in to kiss him. His lips were soft, sweet. He didn't try to back away or make an excuse for why we shouldn't be kissing.

I knew what last night was. We didn't talk about it.

It happened. It was over.

It probably wouldn't be repeated, but still Smoke kissed me, still seemed to like that.

CHELLE BLISS & EDEN BUTLER

I ended the kiss first, smiling at how he watched me, liking the way he held my face, how those steely eyes seemed to soak up every inch of my face. **"Beautiful,"** he said.

"Thank you, *papi*. You're not so bad yourself."

He had a great smile. Wide and welcoming, warm and friendly, and in the right mood, very tempting. "You'll take the gifts? And the job? We'll get you set up and away from the shitty job and the shitty manager you were telling Antonia about."

"She told you?"

"Maggie, one thing you gotta know. This family? Fuck thinking you can keep anything secret. I know about him screwing you on your check. I know about your friend and her asshole of a husband." Smoke laughed when I covered my mouth. He pulled my hand down, looping our fingers together. "I can't promise to be your man." He looked at Mateo, and there was something in his eyes, something that made my chest ache that Smoke blinked away quickly. "I can't be his father, but I can have your back and look out for you. You need that. You need a friend and I got you. You understand me?"

Smoke was serious. His grip was tight on my hand, his expression fierce. And in that moment, with my sweet baby sleeping against me, I knew there was hope that not all good men had disappeared from the world. Even the ones who were only sort of good.

"I understand you, *papi*."

"Good," he said, moving close to plant a soft, sweet kiss on my wrist. "Then take this, all of this. And when he wakes up, let's give your boy the best first Christmas any kid's ever had."

"Yes. I'd like that."

I got the feeling, in this small town, I'd be saying that a lot.

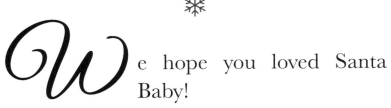 e hope you loved Santa Baby!

Smoke and Maggie are just getting started and so is the Carelli family!

Want to know when the next Carelli novel releases?

Please visit menofinked.com/bliss-butler and sign up for a new release alert!

While you're waiting, there's more Chelle Bliss & Eden Butler waiting to be read!

- Book 1 - Nailed Down

- Book 2 - Tied Down (Cara Carelli)
- Book 3 - Kneel Down
- Book 4 - Stripped Down (Johnny Carelli)

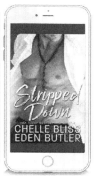

Do you LOVE audiobooks?

The entire Nailed Down series is now available in audiobook.

Santa Baby is coming to Audio too!

ABOUT EDEN BUTLER

Eden Butler is an editor and writer of Romance, SciFi and Fantasy novels and the nine-time great-granddaughter of an honest-to-God English pirate. This could explain her affinity for rule breaking and rum.

When she's not writing, or wondering about her *possibly* Jack Sparrowesque ancestor, Eden impatiently awaits her Hogwarts letter, writes, reads and spends too much time watching New Orleans Saints football, and dreaming up plots that will likely keep her on deadline until her hair is white and her teeth are missing.

Currently, she is imprisoned under teenage rule alongside her husband in Southeastern Louisiana. Please send help.

WEBSITE – edenbutler.com
READER GROUP – https://
bit.ly/2kzMnsf

Subscribe to Eden's newsletter http://
eepurl.com/VXQXD for giveaways,
sneak peeks and various goodies that
might just give you a chuckle.

ABOUT CHELLE BLISS

Chelle Bliss is the *Wall Street Journal* and *USA Today* bestselling author of Men of Inked: Southside Series, Misadventures of a City Girl, the Men of Inked, and ALFA Investigations series.

She hails from the Midwest, but currently lives near the beach even though she hates sand. She's a full-time writer, time-waster extraordinaire, social media addict, coffee fiend, and ex history teacher.

She loves spending time with her two cats, alpha boyfriend, and chatting with readers. To learn more about Chelle, please visit menofinked.com.

JOIN MY NEWSLETTER

Text Notifications (US only)
→ Text **BLISS** to **24587**

WHERE TO FOLLOW CHELLE:

WEBSITE | TWITTER |
FACEBOOK | INSTAGRAM
JOIN MY PRIVATE FACEBOOK
GROUP

Want to drop me a line?
authorchellebliss@gmail.com
www.chellebliss.com

facebook.com/authorchellebliss1

bookbub.com/authors/chelle-bliss

instagram.com/authorchellebliss

twitter.com/ChelleBliss1

Made in the USA
Coppell, TX
06 December 2019